NEW YORK
JETS

BY SAULIE BLUMBERG

SportsZone

An Imprint of Abdo Publishing
abdopublishing.com

abdopublishing.com

Published by Abdo Publishing, a division of ABDO, PO Box 398166, Minneapolis, Minnesota 55439. Copyright © 2017 by Abdo Consulting Group, Inc. International copyrights reserved in all countries. No part of this book may be reproduced in any form without written permission from the publisher. SportsZone™ is a trademark and logo of Abdo Publishing.

Printed in the United States of America, North Mankato, Minnesota
042016
092016

Cover Photo: David Drapkin/AP Images
Interior Photos: David Drapkin/AP Images, 1; AP Images, 4-5, 14; NFL Photos/AP Images, 6; Vernon J. Biever/AP Images, 7, 12-13, 15; John Lindsay/AP Images, 8-9; Al Messerschmidt/AP Images, 10-11, 24-25; Bill Kostroun/AP Images, 16-17, 20-21; Paul Sakuma/AP Images, 18-19; Andrew J. Cohoon, 22-23; Greg Trott/AP Images, 26-27; Peter Morgan/AP Images, 28; Evan Pinkus/AP Images, 29

Editor: Todd Kortemeier
Series Designer: Nikki Farinella

Cataloging-in-Publication Data
Names: Blumberg, Saulie, author.
Title: New York Jets / by Saulie Blumberg.
Description: Minneapolis, MN : Abdo Publishing, [2017] | Series: NFL up close | Includes index.
Identifiers: LCCN 2015960441 | ISBN 9781680782271 (lib. bdg.) | ISBN 9781680776386 (ebook)
Subjects: LCSH: New York Jets (Football team)--History--Juvenile literature. | National Football League--Juvenile literature. | Football--Juvenile literature. | Professional sports--Juvenile literature. | Football teams--New York--Juvenile literature.
Classification: DDC 796.332--dc23
LC record available at http://lccn.loc.gov/2015960441

TABLE OF CONTENTS

THE GUARANTEE

Joe Namath said they would do it. The star quarterback was speaking to the press at the Miami Touchdown Club in Florida. It was January 9, 1969, three days before the New York Jets played the powerful Baltimore Colts in the third Super Bowl.

Few thought the Jets could win. The Colts were champions of the National Football League (NFL) and were favored by 19 points. The Jets won the American Football League (AFL), seen at the time as an inferior league. Someone in the audience told Namath the Jets had no chance. He had a strong reply.

"We'll win," he said. "I guarantee it."

Jets quarterback Joe Namath knew he'd have to play well to make good on his guarantee.

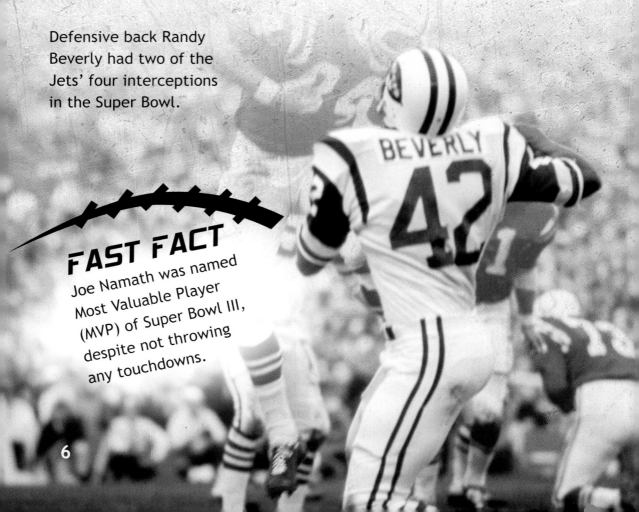

Namath and the Jets might have been the only ones who believed his words. But that Sunday at the Orange Bowl, Namath outplayed Baltimore's strong defense. New York's defense held the mighty Colts to one touchdown. The final score was Jets 16, Colts 7.

For the first time, the AFL beat the NFL in the Super Bowl. That made fans realize that the newer AFL might be just as good as the NFL. In 1970, the two leagues merged into one. Namath and the Jets were one of the AFL's most memorable teams.

Defensive back Randy Beverly had two of the Jets' four interceptions in the Super Bowl.

FAST FACT

Joe Namath was named Most Valuable Player (MVP) of Super Bowl III, despite not throwing any touchdowns.

6

Running back Matt Snell scored the Jets' only touchdown.

FAST FACT

Receiver Don Maynard was the first player the Titans signed. He became the second Jets player to make the Pro Football Hall of Fame.

Sammy Baugh, *standing*, poses with the rest of the Titans' first coaching staff in 1960.

FROM TITANS TO JETS

The NFL began playing in 1920. Forty years later, in 1960, the AFL began with eight teams. The Titans were one of those original teams. They played in New York City. Sammy Baugh, who had been one of the NFL's greatest quarterbacks, was their coach.

They played home games at the Polo Grounds. It was a famous baseball stadium where the New York Giants and Yankees once played. Built in 1883, it was already very old by the time the Titans began playing there.

FAST FACT

In 1963, the Jets hired Weeb Ewbank as coach. Ewbank became the only coach to win championships in both the NFL and AFL.

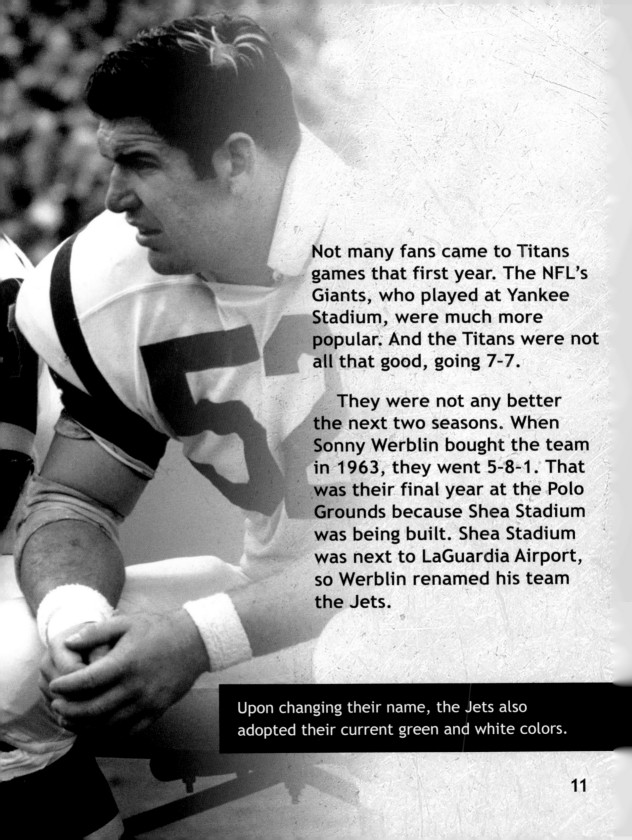

Not many fans came to Titans games that first year. The NFL's Giants, who played at Yankee Stadium, were much more popular. And the Titans were not all that good, going 7-7.

They were not any better the next two seasons. When Sonny Werblin bought the team in 1963, they went 5-8-1. That was their final year at the Polo Grounds because Shea Stadium was being built. Shea Stadium was next to LaGuardia Airport, so Werblin renamed his team the Jets.

Upon changing their name, the Jets also adopted their current green and white colors.

BROADWAY JOE YEARS

"Broadway Joe" Namath was the Jets' first star. The team drafted him first overall in 1965. Both the AFL and NFL wanted Namath. He signed a $427,000 contract, a huge amount of money at the time, to play in the AFL.

Namath was one of the most popular football players ever. He had a strong arm and played with a confidence that fans loved. He often wore flashy white shoes instead of the usual black during games. His popularity was a main reason the AFL merged with the NFL in 1970.

FAST FACT

Joe Namath later became an actor and broadcaster. He appeared in several movies and TV shows.

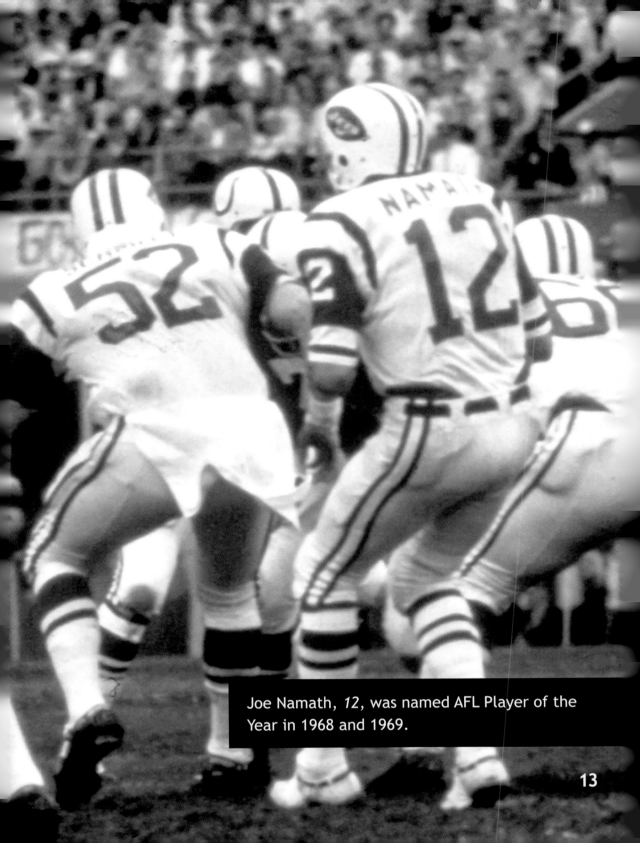

Joe Namath, *12*, was named AFL Player of the
Year in 1968 and 1969.

Namath's favorite receiver was Don Maynard, who played 13 seasons with the Jets. Weeb Ewbank became the Jets coach in 1963. He led the Baltimore Colts to the 1958 NFL title. He and the Jets upset his old team in the Super Bowl after the 1968 season.

In 1970, the AFL and NFL joined together. The Jets struggled at first in the new NFL. Namath missed many games due to injury. After Ewbank retired in 1973, the team tried five different coaches from 1974 to 1977. None were able to bring the Jets back to the playoffs.

The Jets played at Shea Stadium until 1984. They shared it with baseball's New York Mets.

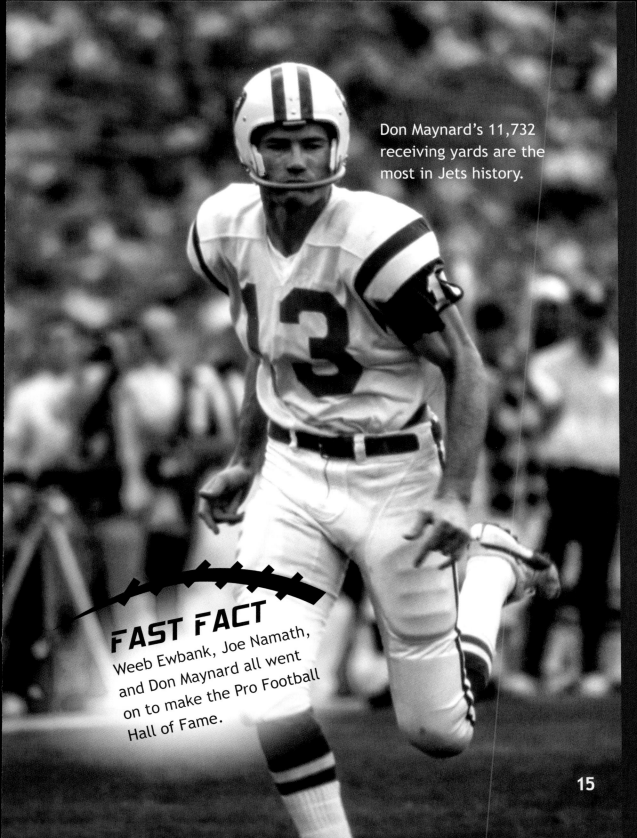

Don Maynard's 11,732 receiving yards are the most in Jets history.

FAST FACT

Weeb Ewbank, Joe Namath, and Don Maynard all went on to make the Pro Football Hall of Fame.

Namath played his last season with the Jets in 1976. He threw only four touchdowns along with 16 interceptions. New York didn't have a winning record for the entire 1970s. A shutdown defense helped the Jets rebound in the early 1980s. They even got to within one game of the Super Bowl in 1982.

The 1983 NFL Draft haunted the Jets for years. They chose quarterback Ken O'Brien over Dan Marino. O'Brien was a good quarterback, and he led the Jets to three playoff appearances. But Marino went on to a Hall of Fame career with the Miami Dolphins. He led the Dolphins to many big wins over the Jets.

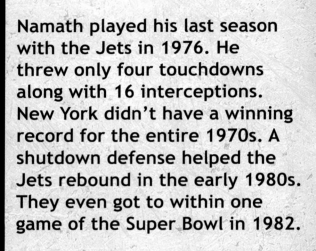

Jets defensive end Mark Gastineau led the NFL with 19 sacks in 1983 and a then-record 22 in 1984.

PRIDE OF HOFSTRA

For years, the Jets practiced at Hofstra University in New York. For most of those seasons, they invited a Hofstra player to try out for the team. Sometimes they even chose that player in the NFL Draft.

In 1995, a receiver from Hofstra named Wayne Chrebet went undrafted. At 5-foot-10 and 185 pounds, teams thought he might be too small to play in the NFL. But Chrebet worked hard, and he earned a spot with the Jets.

FAST FACT

Three other Hofstra players went on to play for the Jets. John Schmitt was the center for the 1969 Super Bowl champs. Willie Colon and Stephen Bowen were the others.

Wayne Chrebet was small, but he made a lot of big catches. In fact, 379 of his 580 career receptions went for first downs.

Chrebet became one of the most popular Jets ever. In 1998, he helped them return to the playoffs. Chrebet hauled in 75 catches for 1,083 yards and eight touchdowns. New running back Curtis Martin had his first of seven seasons with more than 1,000 rushing yards.

The 1998 Jets won 12 games, the most in team history. Their playoff run got them to within one game of the Super Bowl. They even held a slim 3-0 halftime lead over the Denver Broncos in the conference championship game. But Denver had a 20-point third quarter to pull away and send the Jets home.

Curtis Martin led the NFL in rushing with 1,697 yards in 2004.

Vinny Testaverde played seven of his 21 NFL seasons with the Jets.

"MONDAY NIGHT MIRACLE"

On October 23, 2000, the Jets played one of the most memorable games in NFL history. They faced the Miami Dolphins on Monday Night Football. They trailed Miami 30-7 in the fourth quarter. Then the comeback began.

Vinny Testaverde threw three touchdown passes on the next four Jets drives. A John Hall field goal on the other drive tied it at 30. But the Dolphins woke up, and they scored on their next offensive play for a 37-30 lead.

FAST FACT

Vinny Testaverde had 378 passing yards and five touchdowns in the Jets' comeback victory over Miami in 2000.

23

The Jets were not finished. With 42 seconds left, they called a rare pass play for offensive lineman Jumbo Elliott. He got open in the end zone. Testaverde threw the ball his way. Elliott bobbled the ball and held on. In overtime, Hall kicked a 34-yard field goal to finish the amazing comeback and win the game 40-37.

Still, the 2000 season did not end in a playoff appearance. The Jets made it in 2001 and again in 2002 with new quarterback Chad Pennington. Pennington never put up big numbers, but he led the Jets to three playoff appearances in the 2000s.

Jumbo Elliott's lone career touchdown catch completed the Jets' "Monday Night Miracle" comeback.

FAST FACT
Rex Ryan's father, Buddy Ryan, won two Super Bowls in his NFL coaching career. One was with the Jets when he was the defensive line coach.

CLOSE CALLS

Rex Ryan became coach of the Jets in 2009. He often spoke his mind. When he came to New York, he said the Jets would never back down or be afraid of any team. That is exactly how they played during his six seasons in charge.

Under Ryan, the Jets had a strong, hard-hitting defense led by such stars as cornerback Darrelle Revis and linebacker David Harris. They blitzed a lot. They got many interceptions and forced a lot of fumbles.

Coach Rex Ryan, *in black vest*, was known for showing emotion on the sidelines.

In his first two seasons, Ryan led the Jets into the playoffs even though they did not win their division. Then they won two playoff road games in 2009 before losing to the Indianapolis Colts in the conference championship. In 2010, they again won two road playoff games before falling to the Pittsburgh Steelers.

Ryan's teams were fun to watch. But he did not have another winning season before being fired in 2014. The Jets bounced back to a 10-6 record in 2015, and they barely missed the playoffs. With talent on offense and defense, the Jets should be competitive for years to come.

FAST FACT

The Jets have shared a stadium with the Giants since 1984, when they moved into Giants Stadium. The two teams currently share MetLife Stadium, which opened in 2010.

MetLife Stadium holds 82,500 fans.

Defensive end Muhammad Wilkerson, 96, had 12 sacks in 2015 and made his first Pro Bowl.

TIMELINE

1960
The New York Titans join seven other teams to form the AFL.

1963
Sonny Werblin buys the team, renames them the Jets, and hires Weeb Ewbank as coach.

1969
Joe Namath guarantees the Jets will beat the 19-point favorite Baltimore Colts in the Super Bowl, and they do, 16-7 on January 12.

1981
The Jets make the playoffs for the first time since becoming a member of the NFL, but they lose to the Buffalo Bills in the first round, 31-27.

1983
The Jets lose to the Miami Dolphins 14-0 in the conference title game on January 23.

1999
With Bill Parcells as coach, the Jets make it to the conference championship game, but they lose to the Denver Broncos 23-10 on January 17.

2000
In the "Monday Night Miracle," the Jets rally for 30 points in the fourth quarter and beat Miami 40-37 in overtime on October 23.

2010
The Jets play in their first conference championship game since 1998 but lose to the Indianapolis Colts, 30-17 on January 24.

2015
The Jets finish 10-6, their first winning record since 2010, but they miss the playoffs.

GLOSSARY

BLITZ
When a defense has more than the usual four or five players rush the quarterback.

COMEBACK
When a team losing a game rallies to win.

CONTRACT
An agreement to play for a certain team.

DIVISION
A group of teams that help form a league.

DRAFT
The process by which teams select players who are new to the league.

FUMBLE
When a player with the ball loses possession, allowing the opponent a chance to recover it.

INTERCEPTION
When a defensive player catches a pass intended for an offensive player.

OVERTIME
An extra period or periods played in the event of a tie.

PLAYOFFS
A set of games played after the regular season that decides which team will be the champion.

INDEX

ABOUT THE AUTHOR

Saulie Blumberg is a freelance sports writer based in suburban New York who hopes to see the Jets play in another Super Bowl.